Why the Sea is Salty

(*A myth from Wales*)

Chapter 1

There were once two brothers named Glyn and Maldwyn who lived in Wales. Glyn was a rich fisherman. He lived in a fine house in a village by the sea. Maldwyn was

a poor farmer. He lived in a small stone hut, high up in the hills. The two brothers hardly ever spoke to each other.

One Christmas, Maldwyn found he had nothing left to eat. He sat shivering and hungry in his stone hut.

• *Glyn:* (say) 'glin'. • *Maldwyn:* (say) 'mold-win'. 3

'There's nothing for it,' he thought. 'I'll have to go and see my brother.'

Maldwyn took the track down from the hills to the village. It was a cold night and a bitter wind was blowing. When he came to his brother's house he saw the windows were lit and he heard loud laughter.

'Glyn must be having a party,' thought Maldwyn. 'Perhaps he'll invite me in.'

He knocked on the door and waited. Then he knocked again. He knocked even louder the third time. The door finally opened.

'Who are you?' asked Glyn, peering into the shadows.

'It's me, Maldwyn.'

'What do you want?' snapped Glyn.

'I have no food,' said Maldwyn.

'I don't give to beggars,' said Glyn.

'But I'm your brother!' said Maldwyn.

Glyn glared at him angrily then slammed the door in his face. Sadly, Maldwyn turned to leave. A few moments later Glyn opened the door again and held out a leg of lamb.

'Have this,' he muttered. 'Then take yourself off to Dead Man's Land.'

The door slammed shut again.

Chapter 2

Maldwyn stood holding the leg of lamb. 'Hmm, Dead Man's Land,' he thought. 'I wonder where that is?'

Maldwyn didn't realise that Glyn just meant he should go away and not come back! He thought about the long, cold journey back home. 'Perhaps it will be an easier journey to Dead Man's Land,' he said to himself and set off.

Near the village there was a river. Maldwyn followed the river inland. It grew wider and deeper and passed between high cliffs. At last, it disappeared into a cave. Maldwyn stood at the entrance to the cave. It echoed with the sound of the water tumbling and gushing.

'I wonder if this is the entrance to Dead Man's Land,' he thought.

The cave was huge. A surge of cold air swept around him.

In the gloom, Maldwyn saw swarms of ghostly figures with pale faces and wide, staring eyes. Their voices were like the rustling of leaves in an autumn wind.

'Who are you?' they said.

'I'm Maldwyn. I'm looking for Dead Man's Land.'

A loud voice echoed through the cave. 'You have found it!' The ghosts glided apart to make way for a tall, cloaked figure. On his head was a crown of bones. Tiny red flames burned in his eyes. It was the King of Dead Man's Land.

He stared at Maldwyn. 'You have meat,' he said. 'What will you take for it?'

'What will you give?' asked Maldwyn.

'Gold, silver, jewels,' said the King. 'Anything you ask.'

'Give me the best thing you have,' said Maldwyn.

The King laughed. Maldwyn shuddered.

The laughter was like icy water being poured down the back of his neck.

'Here,' said the King. He drew something from beneath his cloak. He held out a small hand-mill. 'Turn the handle and the mill will grind out anything you wish for. When you want it to stop just say the word *Enough*.'

Maldwyn took the mill from the King. He
wished for some stew and turned the handle.
Immediately, stew started pouring out of the
grinder onto the floor of the cave.

Maldwyn was so hungry that he dropped to
his knees and scooped the stew into his mouth.
He ate until he was full, but then he saw that
the mill was still grinding out stew.

'Enough!' he cried. The mill stopped.

Maldwyn wiped his mouth and looked around him. The cave was empty. The King and the ghostly figures had vanished. Maldwyn picked up the mill and made his way home.

Now Maldwyn had plenty to eat for the rest of Christmas and every day after too. Whenever he was hungry, he just wished for what it was he wanted to eat, turned the handle of the mill, and out it came.

Chapter 3

As time passed, people noticed how well-fed and happy Maldwyn looked. Soon, Glyn came to hear of it and he was puzzled. Had his brother come into some money? He decided to go and find out.

Maldwyn was surprised when he saw Glyn standing in his doorway. He was grinding himself a tea-time treat from the hand-mill – Welsh cakes. They smelled delicious.

Glyn stared at the marvellous, magic mill. 'Where did you get this?' he said.

Maldwyn told him the story of his journey to Dead Man's Land.

'I want to buy it from you,' said Glyn. 'Name your price.'

'It's not for sale,' said Maldwyn.

Glyn tried again and again to persuade Maldwyn to sell the mill, but Maldwyn refused. At last, Glyn appeared to give up.

'All right,' he said. 'But let me borrow it for a few days.'

Maldwyn wasn't sure about this.

'Trust me,' said Glyn. 'After all, if I hadn't told you to go to Dead Man's Land, you wouldn't have the mill.'

Maldwyn had to agree with this, so he let his brother borrow the mill.

Glyn hurried back to his village. He wasn't going to return the mill to Maldwyn. He planned to make a lot of money from it.

Chapter 4

Across the sea there was a great city with a large fish market. Glyn had always wanted to sell his fish at that market, because he could charge twice the usual price. He had never done this because the city was so far away that he could not keep his fish fresh enough on the journey. Now he had the mill, Glyn knew he could grind out as much salt as he needed to keep his fish fresh.

The next day he packed his boat with his nets and set sail. When he was out of sight of land he cast his nets into the sea. Before long he was hauling them back in, filled with the biggest, finest fish. Now it was time to pack them in salt, then settle back to enjoy the rest of the journey. Glyn wished for the mill to grind salt, and turned the handle. The mill began to grind.

17

When there was enough salt for all the fish
Glyn told the mill to stop. 'Stop, now,' he said,
but the mill carried on grinding. 'I said, stop!'
But it didn't stop. It carried on. 'No more!' he
cried. 'STOP IT! PLEASE, PLEASE,
PLEASE STOP!'

But the mill carried on grinding.
Glyn shouted everything he
could think of, except for that
one magic word *Enough*.

Soon, the boat was filled
with salt. The boat's planks
began to creak and split. Then,
with a splintering crash, the planks burst under
the weight of the salt. The sea gushed in. The
boat, the fish, Glyn and the mill, all sank.

Maldwyn never saw the mill or his brother again. He left his small stone hut and went to live in his brother's fine house. He became a fisherman and lived comfortably for the rest of his days.

As for the mill, down on the sea-bed, it carried on grinding out salt. Soon, the sea began to taste of it. To this very day, the mill is still grinding, and that is why the sea is salty.

Indra and Vritra

Chapter 1

Deep inside a mountain there lived a dragon. He had been there since the beginning of time, sleeping in his cave, dreaming his terrible dragon dreams. The people who lived nearby had no idea that the dragon was there.

Until one day, there was a rumbling in the ground.

• *Indra:* (say) 'in-druh'. • *Vritra:* (say) 'vrit-ruh'.

The mountain began to shake. Rocks came tumbling and crashing down the slopes.

The people cried out in terror. They wanted to run and hide, but where can you hide from a falling mountain?

The rumbling grew louder. There was a thundering, grinding sound, as a great crack opened in the mountain and a huge creature flew out.

It was Vritra, the most powerful and terrible of all dragons.

The people were rooted to the ground with fear. They watched Vritra fly up into the sky, beating the air with his massive wings. They stared at his wide head and four curved horns. They gasped at his great jaws filled with rows of sharp teeth, and his long tail that whipped the air. His whole body glittered with scales of red and gold.

After stretching his wings, Vritra dropped back down to the mountain. His head rested on the mountain-top, the tip of his tail flicked among the trees. He gazed across the whole of India. Everywhere, he saw the same thing. People! People fishing in the rivers, working in the fields, talking to each other, singing, laughing.

His eyes burned like two fierce flames and he gave a long, loud hiss.

This is what had woken him – the sound of people living their lives. These sounds were awful to him. He wanted the earth to be silent again. He stared at all the rivers and lakes shining in the sunlight. An idea flashed into his evil mind.

Hissssssssssssssssss . . .

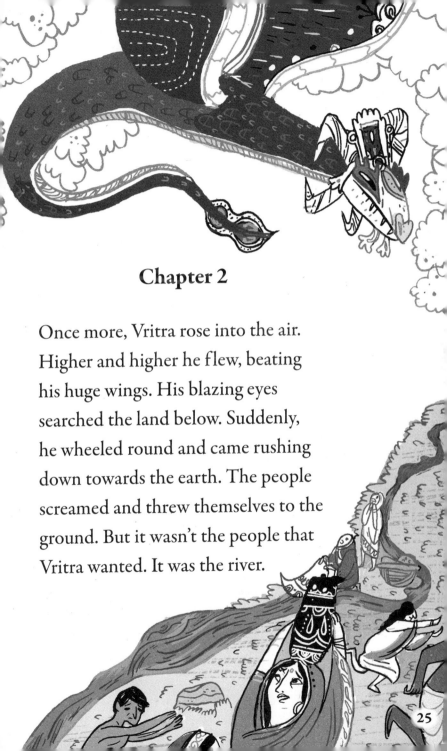

Chapter 2

Once more, Vritra rose into the air.
Higher and higher he flew, beating
his huge wings. His blazing eyes
searched the land below. Suddenly,
he wheeled round and came rushing
down towards the earth. The people
screamed and threw themselves to the
ground. But it wasn't the people that
Vritra wanted. It was the river.

Vritra lay on the bank. He opened his jaws wide and sucked up the whole river into his vast stomach. Soon, the river was just a muddy channel.

Then Vritra soared up again into the sky and set off across India. He stopped at every river, every brook, every lake, every pool, even the tiniest puddles. He drank them all. When he'd finished, India was as dry as an old bone.

Vritra flew
north. His vast
body was swollen with all
the water. His wings strained
and stretched to carry his
bloated body. At last, he came to
a land of mountains. Their peaks
scraped the sky. Freezing winds blasted
and howled around their steep, craggy sides.
Vritra found a valley that lay deep among those
mountains and settled there to sleep. He was sure
he had found peace again.

Chapter 3

All across India the sun beat fiercely upon the land. The earth became dry and cracked. Leaves crumpled on the trees. Plants, grasses and trees died. Animals died. Soon, the people would begin to die too. They prayed to the gods.

'Please help us!' they cried in their dry, croaking voices. 'Don't let the land die! Send someone to bring the water back!'

Indra heard them. He was
the strongest of the gods and a great
hero. He raced across the sky in his golden
chariot. His body gleamed a deep red in the
sunlight. He held a bow in his hand. In his belt
was a curved sword and a dagger. A large net
was slung across his shoulders. He wasn't going
to let India and its people die. Indra was going
to bring back the water.

Chapter 4

When Indra came to the land of mountains, he looked down from his chariot. Vritra was curled up asleep in his deep valley. He knew he could not fight the dragon down there. He needed more space.

Indra pulled on the reins and turned the horses. The chariot sped down towards the mountains. As he drew near, Indra drew his sword and with a single blow he sliced off one of the mountain peaks. Then another, and another, and another. They crashed down into the valley.

Vritra woke. Rocks were falling all around him. He looked up and saw Indra in his golden chariot, slashing at the mountains.

Each sweep of the blade made the mountains smaller. Soon there would be none left! Vritra's eyes blazed with rage. He spread his wings and with a loud and terrible roar, flew into the air.

This was what Indra was waiting for.

He put down his sword, grabbed his bow
and sent an arrow flying towards the
dragon. The arrow bounced off the scales,
and so did the next one and the next.

When Indra had no arrows left, he
took up his sword again.
He charged at the
dragon. As they met,
Indra swung his
chariot around
and struck at the
monster's neck. But
the sword bounced
off Vritra's scales
and flew out of
Indra's hand.

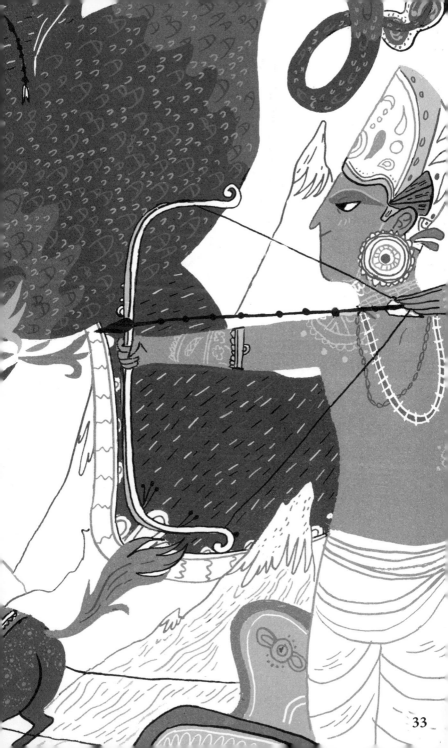

33

It was the same when he flung his dagger. Then, when Indra threw his net over Vritra's head, the dragon just tore it to pieces with his razor teeth.

Soon, the only thing left in Indra's chariot was a large silver jug. Inside this jug was a magic drink called soma. One mouthful would make Indra twice as strong. He drank the whole jug! The power of the soma flowed through his body. With a great shout, Indra raced his chariot high into the air. The thundering of its wheels and the horses' hooves made the mountains shake. Dark clouds gathered. Lightning cracked. Indra reached out and took hold of two lightning bolts. He gave another shout and the horses plunged downwards again.

Indra charged towards Vritra. Vritra roared,
his jaws greedy for Indra. His vast mouth
slavered and his serpent tongue lashed out.
Indra hurled the lightning bolts, one, two,
and they shot between the dragon's jaws
and down his throat. There was a
mighty crash, a flash of flame, and
Vritra the dragon was blasted
to pieces.

All the waters that Vritra had swallowed
gushed out of his broken body. They tumbled
out of his mouth and flooded over the land.
The rivers and streams flowed again. The lakes
and pools filled. The thirsty roots of plants and
trees drank the water as it sank into the earth.

Indra looked down from his chariot and smiled. He saw the land slowly turning green again and knew that his job was done.

The people laughed and clapped their hands with joy. They danced and sang in praise of Indra. He had brought the land back to life.

Sedna

A myth from the Arctic

Chapter 1

In the far north of the world, in a land of ice and snow, there lived a girl named Sedna. She lived alone with her father, and helped him with his fishing and hunting. Sedna was very beautiful. She had long black hair which she liked her father to comb as she sat before the fire.

One clear, cold morning, Sedna was cleaning the fish her father had caught. Her father sat nearby, sharpening his harpoon.

As Sedna turned to hang the fish out to dry, she saw a figure walking across the snow.

'Look,' she said. 'We have a visitor.'

Her father looked up. 'I don't think I know this man,' he said.

The figure was dressed in a robe of thick fur. A large hood hung over his face. There was something odd about the way he held his body. His shoulders were hunched and his head bent forward. There was a croak in his voice when he spoke.

'I'm looking for a wife,' he said to Sedna's father. 'I've been told that your daughter is very beautiful. Now that I've seen her, I know it is true.'

'Who are you?' Sedna's father asked
the stranger.

'I am a great chief,' he said. 'My land is across
the sea. If Sedna will come with me and be my
wife, she will be well looked after. There are
many riches in my country.'

Sedna looked at the stranger. He was
mysterious but she could see his eyes
glimmering under the shadow of the hood.
Sedna liked the idea of being a chief's wife in a
rich country. So when her father looked at her,
she smiled and nodded.

Chapter 2

Sedna quickly packed then said goodbye to her father. Her new husband's kayak was waiting on the shore.

The chief rowed the kayak across the icy sea.

Before long, Sedna saw an island. In the distance, it just looked like a lump of bare, jagged rock. As they got closer, Sedna gasped. The island really was just a lump of bare, jagged rock!

As they climbed out of the kayak, there was a harsh laugh behind her. She turned and let out a cry of horror.

It wasn't a human face that looked back at her. It was the face of a giant raven. Sedna tried to jump back into the kayak but the raven grabbed her in his beak. He dragged her to a craggy peak where there was a nest of dry twigs and fish bones.

'This is your home from now on,' croaked the raven. 'Enjoy your meal!' he cackled. Then he flew away.

Sedna looked about her. The peak was too steep for her to climb down. She was stranded. There was one raw fish in the nest. It was the only food. Sedna began to cry.

Chapter 3

That night, an icy wind swirled around the island. Sedna sat in the nest, shivering. In her misery she called out to her father. The wind sucked up her voice and carried it across the wild, rolling waves.

The wind blew Sedna's voice into her father's dreams. He woke up knowing that his daughter was in trouble. He ran down to his kayak and set out to rescue her.

By dawn, Sedna's father
had reached the island.
He saw Sedna stranded on
the rocky peak so he threw
up a strong, thick fishing line.
Sedna tied the line to some
rocks and used it to climb
down into her father's boat.
She hugged him, sobbing.
'Please take me home,'
she begged.
The kayak hadn't gone
far before there was a
heavy beating of wings,
and a dark shadow
passed over them.
It was the raven!

He swooped down, grabbing for Sedna with his beak. Sedna's father struck him with his oar.

The raven shrieked and flew up again. Then he swooped down over the sea, beating at the waves with his wings, whipping them into a terrible storm. The kayak rolled from side to side, pounded by the heaving ocean. Suddenly a mighty wave crashed over the kayak. Sedna was flung into the icy sea.

Sedna struggled back towards the kayak, and grasped its side. Her father reached down to help her, but Sedna's hands and fingers had frozen. When he took hold of them they snapped off and dropped into the ocean. With a cry Sedna fell back and was sucked beneath the waves.

The raven gave a croak of victory and flew back to his island. With a heavy heart, Sedna's father paddled his kayak back home.

Chapter 4

Time passed but a deep gloom spread over the seas. Sedna's father went out fishing but he caught less and less. It was the same for the other fishermen. Families went hungry. They began to starve.

One night, Sedna's father dreamed his daughter was calling to him. In his dream, he set off in his kayak to look for her. At first the sea was calm but when he looked into the water he saw strange creatures. They were large, grey, whiskery creatures with tails and flippers.

They began to knock against his kayak. He was terrified. The kayak rocked backwards and forwards until it tipped up and Sedna's father was plunged into the water.

He sank down, deeper and deeper, until he reached the sea bed. There, to his amazement, he found Sedna.

She was changed. She still had her human face and her long hair but her body was that of a seal. Her broken off fingers had become these new creatures, the seals, the walruses, and the great whales. She had power over these creatures and power over the sea itself.

Sedna was now goddess of the sea.

Yet it did not make her happy. She was sad and lonely and that's why she had kept the fish at the bottom of the sea with her. Sedna's father listened to his daughter. He soothed her sadness by combing her long hair, as he used to do. He told her that people were starving and begged her to let all the fish and creatures of the sea swim freely again.

At last Sedna agreed, but only if her father made a promise. He had to promise that whenever she was lonely, a man would come down to her kingdom to keep her company and comb out her hair.

When Sedna's father woke he knew it had not been an ordinary dream. He took out his kayak and found the seas once more filled with fish, and those strange new creatures, the seals and walruses.

The people of the north
say that Sedna is still there,
deep down on the sea bed.
When she's happy the fish
and creatures of the sea
swim freely. But when
she is lonely, the sea
seems empty.

Then a man must
go, in his dreams,
beneath the sea.
He must find
Sedna, comb
out her hair and
remind her of life
in the upper world.